# TULIP SEES AMERICA

## CYNTHIA RYLANT

illustrations by

# LISA DESIMINI

SCHOLASTIC INC.

New York  Toronto  London  Auckland  Sydney
Mexico City  New Delhi  Hong Kong  Buenos Aires

This book was originally published in hardcover by the Blue Sky Press in 1998.

ISBN 0-439-39978-5

Text copyright © 1998 by Cynthia Rylant.
Illustrations copyright © 1998 by Lisa Desimini.
All rights reserved.
Published by Scholastic Inc. SCHOLASTIC and associated logos
are trademarks and/or registered trademarks of Scholastic Inc.

12 11 10                                        11 12 13 14/0

Printed in the United States of America                    40

First Scholastic trade paperback printing, May 2002

Designed by Kathleen Westray and Lisa Desimini

To Leia and Martha Jane,
for being such good dogs
on our trip
— C. R.

For my nephew,
James
— L. D.

**W**hen I was a boy,

I didn't see much of America.

My parents were homebodies,

so I stayed home.

But when I grew up,
I knew I was different.
I wanted to see America.

So I bought a little green Beetle and in it I put a small box of clothes, a small bag of food, and my dog, Tulip.

And we left Ohio
and went across America.

This is what we saw:

The farms in Iowa. They are pictures:
White houses. Red roofs.

Green, green rolling hills
and black garden soil all around them.

Farms like castles in a fairyland,
serene in the morning fog.

There are no farms like Iowa's.

The skies in Nebraska.

They are everything.

They are vast and dark and low and ominous.

And a tiny Beetle feels even tinier,

driving beneath them.

It feels a little afraid.

Then the skies break open

into blue and white and yellow and pink,

and it is like one great long breath

of freedom and air.

There are no skies like Nebraska's.

The wind in Wyoming.
Everything flaps.

Tulip's ears flapped all the way across Wyoming.
And when we stopped to get out of the Beetle,
the wind filled our noses and watered our eyes
and Tulip was ready to get back into the car.

There is no wind like Wyoming's.

The mountains in Colorado.

They are all rock.
Piles of rock as high as the sky
and a river running under them.
Tulip saw a ram on the rocks
and barked for half an hour.

She barked all over those mountains.
At elk. At wolves. At deer.
Our little Beetle puffed like an old man,
driving up and up.

There are no mountains like Colorado's

The desert in Nevada.

There is no place to hide in a desert, and you are glad you are not a rabbit or a mouse someone might want to eat. The desert runs so far and so wide that you think if you are there too long, you will go crazy.

Its flowers are strange and beautiful, and
Tulip chased salamanders between its rocks.

Tulip and I did silly things
we would do only in Nevada.

I took all my clothes off.

I don't know why.
Because no one was there.

Tulip wasn't as silly.
She just dug a big hole for no reason.

There is no desert like Nevada's.

The ocean in Oregon.

You drive up a winding mountain road

and you think there is no ocean anywhere.

You drive between a stand of firs

and you think: no ocean.

Then you blink, and there it is:

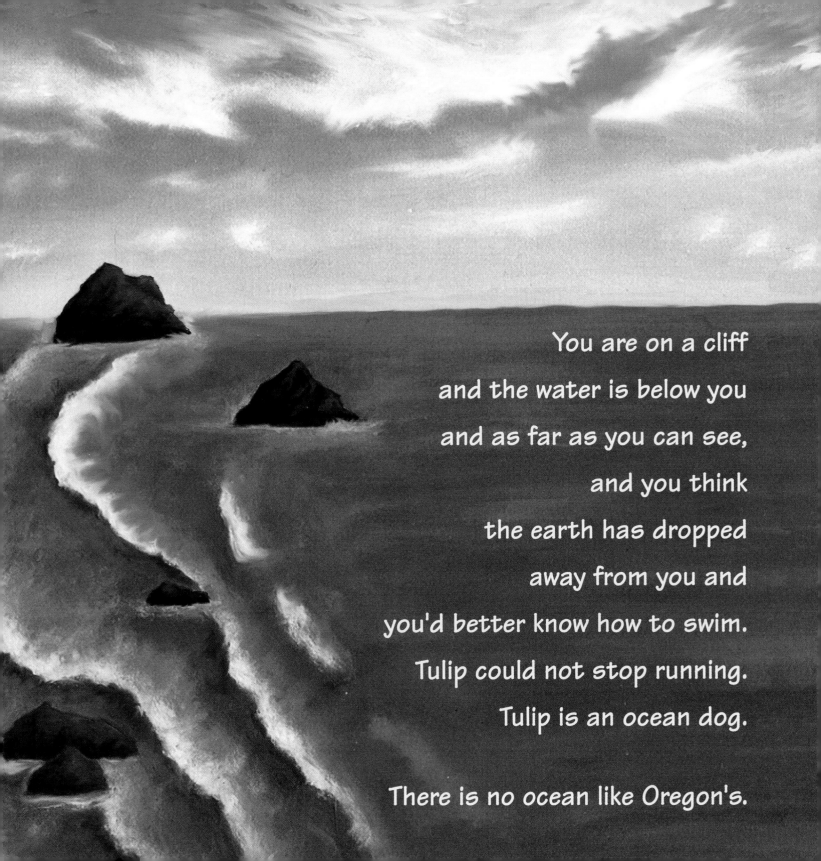

You are on a cliff

and the water is below you

and as far as you can see,

and you think

the earth has dropped

away from you and

you'd better know how to swim.

Tulip could not stop running.

Tulip is an ocean dog.

There is no ocean like Oregon's.

And this is where we stayed.